Loud Silence

Carina Christo

Loud Silence

Loud Silence

By Carina Christo

ISBN 10: 1532758545

ISBN 13: 9781532758546

Published by: Loud Silence, Medfield, MA 02052

Library of Congress Control Number: 2016907253

Printed in the United States of America

First printing January, 2017

Book Design: Carina Christo

Cover Illustration: CreateSpace and Canva.com

Author Photograph: Lisa McDonald

To contact the author for speaking engagements, press, and other inquiries: christocarina@gmail.com

To Andrew

Emma Christ

2019 :)

Loud Silence

For my family and teachers, who have been supporting and inspiring me forever. Also, to all the introverts who are more comfortable speaking on paper than in front of a crowded classroom.

Chapter 1

Every day starts the same, with each awakening virtually alike. Then again, it's all the parts in the middle that really matter. There is adventure in knowing that when you return to sleep, your life will have been altered, even if the change is slight. "Each decision is like a fork in the road, and each event is a new path." That's a quote on one of the posters plastered with peeling masking tape on the walls of my eighth-grade honors English classroom. I copied it into my notebook on the first day of school, back in September, and even that was a fork in the road.

So far, the decisions I've made and the things I've seen haven't led me very far. Then again, I'm only fourteen. But I feel like everyone deserves a miracle at some point. It doesn't matter if it's good or bad, as long as it's a miracle nonetheless. The issue here is that we have no way of knowing when that fateful day will come.

There were no storm clouds warning me of the tempest to come that day, even if the weatherman had said it might rain. But I don't mean literal rain. I'm talking about life's abnormalities washing over me like a tsunami, with no sign of their coming. While that March morning had started normally, or at least practically normal, their effects would last longer than the demolition of any storm. I guess everything's relative.

The sun rose in golden streams through the wooden plantation shutters in my room. Rain added to the dewdrops, which were hugging blades of yellow grass and seeing the sun for the first time after months of icy blizzards wafting past my window.

I guess all my days had a similarity to them, but I tried not to think about that too much. It hurt my brain when I imagined the countless days in front of me, all of them the same. My routine consisted of the *joys* of awkward junior high, where I sat at the same seat for lunch and wore similar outfits every day. Each afternoon I came home to write and eat dinner, which was usually pizza or Chinese, and then watch reruns of Friends or hold my breath at whatever medical show I was binge-watching on Netflix.

I stretched my arms high above my head until I could feel my muscles pull and my bones crack, squinting my eyes as I yawned on the side of my bed. The blood rushed to my head, and I gripped the soft quilt to keep from becoming too dizzy. When I opened them, my vision was blurry, and fuzzy blue spots came and went until I adjusted.

I could hear the muffled strokes of the bow gliding across my brother's cello through the wall, which was covered in a collage of photographs of famous authors at work as well as a few of my best friend Summer and me. His practicing didn't bother me though, even if it was a few minutes after six in the morning.

I thought I woke up early, but my brother woke up even earlier. He practiced in times of darkness melting to a piercing sunrise and in the minutes when the shadows snaked through every corner, discounting the red flashing glow of a digital clock. Those were the times mom and dad couldn't tell him for the last time to finish his homework, which he had usually already finished. Those were his times, though I knew he should've been sitting under floodlights in a crisp suit, playing a grand piano, or strumming a simple acoustic guitar on a stage in front of a sea of fans.

My parents were whispering something about him in the kitchen downstairs. I couldn't hear exactly what they were saying. It was just murmurs, like the sound of chords echoing softly through the barrier of posters. I figured it was about my brother. That's all they ever talked about. In a way, that was good because they didn't notice me as much, and that's exactly what I needed. My parents weren't mean or neglectful or anything. But they didn't understand, and sometimes just understanding is the most important thing anyone can do.

They stopped talking in an anxious halt when I came into the kitchen, wearing my blue flannel pajama pants and oversized long-sleeved T-shirt with a pulled thread that I liked to tug at. They knew that I defended my brother. I just don't know why they didn't. I poured some milk into a bowl of sugary cereal in a lethargic manner, my hair falling out of the lazy attempt I'd made at a french braid. I could still taste the mint toothpaste smeared around my mouth when I licked my chapped lips while I sat down at the granite table, and waited for them to whisper something about Elliott again, but surprisingly, they didn't.

My mom yelled for him to come eat breakfast, but he didn't hear her. He didn't hear much of anything else when he was playing whether it was cello, piano, violin, or the trumpet. Sometimes I wondered what it would be like to actually play an instrument. I wondered if the songs felt different that way. Mostly I wondered if I would be as devoted and dedicated as Elliott. My Aunt Carol tried to teach me some of the different types of notes when I was little, but I grew impatient just waiting to whack some drums and would run away to play with her dog.

When Elliott's practicing, his face always looks so peaceful, yet focused and concentrated; it reminds me of my face when I'm writing. I like to imagine that if someone took a picture of me writing without me knowing, that's what I would look like.

Chapter 2

My mom went upstairs and knocked on Elliott's door for a while before he opened it.

"Come eat breakfast, Elliott. You only have ten minutes if you want to drive Cassidy to school," she yelled.

He hollered back, "OK, OK. Just a sec, Ma."

Even from downstairs I could tell his peaceful expression was gone. I could tell without even looking that his comfort and calmness had faded in an instant, like a wave washing over an elaborate sandcastle.

Running downstairs with thundering footsteps from his black Nikes, he took a Cliff bar and a sticky handful of Honey Nut Cheerios into his old, beat-up Volvo with the dangling headlight, which he bought when he turned sixteen last year. Aunt Carol paid for half, even though she "wasn't doing too well" with the singing stuff. But I guess she didn't like all my dad's life lessons for us kids about work ethic and whatever. So, I sat shotgun, and threw my backpack into the leather back seat patched up with duct tape by the last owner. I tied my Converse up over my socks, which reached halfway up my calves under my faded and ripped jeans. Elliott chuckled under his breath, even though he should have been used to my crazy socks by now. They were covered in pictures of purple llamas, which was perfectly normal compared to some of my other pairs.

I kept my notebook on my lap. I couldn't risk putting it in my backpack, where my lunch box of yogurt and a sloppy peanut butter and honey sandwich could spill or glue from an art project might make the pages stick together.

I bring my notebook everywhere. Most people don't even notice it or think it's anything special, but I know better. Well, it's not really the spiral-bound notebook itself—with its feeble pages that fall out easily that's so special; it's the words inside of it. I've heard people talk about trying to be "more than the sum of their parts"; I try to be more than someone who scratches lines of black ink onto lined paper during algebra. I may only be in eighth grade, but I am a writer. Sure, I'm not published or anything—yet—but I write, and I think that makes me enough of a writer to call myself one.

I write a lot of things in my journal. It's not always stories but includes observations about people, poems, and messy first drafts of my section in the school newspaper. Really, any words go. I even quite literally collect words. Sometimes I jot down a new oxymoron I've just thought of. I find obscure definitions from dusty dictionaries and scribble them into the book. And as I hunt for these words, I find that the rarest gems are the most specific. It's like they know me. They're the thoughts I can't put into words until I find a whole book of others just like them. For example: *jouska*—a hypothetical conversation played in one's mind; *opia*—the vulnerability of looking someone in the eyes; *petrichor*—the aroma of earth after rainfall; and *vellichor*—the strange wistfulness of old bookstores. I have a ton of others, but the one that represented me best was *logophile*—a lover of words.

"Are you doing anything fun in school today?" Elliott asked sarcastically with a crooked smile, even though he knew I was dreading an exam I had been forcing him to help me study for all week long. Usually I didn't even stress too much about tests, but this one counted for 15 percent of my grade, and I was right on the edge of a B-plus and an A-minus, which was a big difference. I just rolled my eyes and peered out the window, past the reflection of my frizzy, untamed light-brown hair—a shade away from being considered dirty blond—and the freckles scattered over my nose and cheeks. I directed my focus to the white pine trees that shook in the wind and the colonial houses that flashed by as I tried to review the terms in my head.

"You want to stop at the café?"

"OK, but we've gotta be quick this time," I answered.

"Oh, please—I barely missed the bell last time," he answered, turning into the dirt parking lot of the familiar breakfast shop, forcing up brown, dusty clouds, and propelling his towers of manila folders to come crashing down. I thought to myself how the ladies in the office had yelled at me for not having a note from my mom or the doctor, but it figures that Elliott the suck-up can get away with anything.

Within five minutes, we'd ordered some chocolate-chip cookies for later, a coffee for Elliott, and a hot chocolate with cinnamon and extra whipped cream for me, making it look like I was drinking coffee too, with a plastic lid and cardboard cozy to keep my hands from burning. These were the only things Elliott would spend his money on. He earned some extra cash from his job working the register at the rustic West Falmouth General Store, now that he really needed to save for college. Still, I felt funny using his money, even though the scent of hot cocoa mixing with the smell of burned chocolate chips and coffee brought a sense of comfort.

Chapter 3

Elliott pulled up to the senior parking lot, telling me to have a good day. Then I walked toward my middle school, which was right next to the high school, with my hands shoved into my pockets because I didn't have gloves or a jacket.

I jogged to my locker, cautious of the teachers who rolled their eyes and groaned before reprimanding us when kids ran in the hallways, even though the hall had been cleared except for those few stragglers who biked to school with rosy cheeks and clouds forming with each heavy breath. I tried to stuff everything inside of my locker so that I could actually close the rusted blue metal door, pushing it with both hands a few times, and then slamming my shoulder against it. I mean it did work, but it kinda hurt and I rubbed the red spot with my hand even though it didn't actually hurt *that* much.

I'm late because of this problem practically every day, but my teachers don't seem to mind. My theory is that they are used to it by now, or they don't get mad because I really do try hard to be a decent student even if I'm not a genius like my brother or the expectations set up for me in the beginning of each year are broken by the time of the first test.

There was a chain of heavy breathing, matching the thickness of the air and I slowly turned my neck, like an owl or a girl in a horror movie, to find that it was Ms. Kahn. She was my English teacher, though I sometimes question just how much crazier the other candidates were when our school was hiring. She came out of nowhere right as I was still grumbling about my shoulder. I jumped, startled with my heart settling back to a normal pace because I hadn't noticed her, and all of a sudden, she told me to come into her classroom. I was supposed to be in History class but she didn't have any first-period classes, since she only taught honors English and newspaper club after school, both of which I was in.

She asked me to sit down, motioning to a red easy chair, which seemed out of place in the empty classroom, cluttered with loose papers fluttering against the pressure of the air conditioner that she kept on all year. Posters were plastered to the walls brimming with quotes that didn't have anything to do with grammar.

She sat down next to me behind her desk, adding another pencil to her bun of dyed light-blond hair and black roots. When she had it pulled back a certain way, I could still see the colors she had dyed it before were blond, with the most miniscule patches of lavender and streaks of turquoise. She was pretty, but in an unconventional kind of way. She never seemed to talk to the other teachers much, but she wasn't mean. Sometimes, if I got to English early after lunch, I saw her writing—like me. I guess Ms. Kahn was a little like me. Even if I might imagine myself differently ten years from now, I could imagine her like me ten years earlier.

I sat at the edge of the soft square cushion, still uncomfortable that I would be late for my test.

"Um, Ms. Kahn—" I said, getting cut off.

"Please, call me Martha." For some reason she didn't seem like a Martha. Maybe something more unique like Isadora or Violet, I don't know—something more fitting.

"Excuse me, um, Martha, can I talk to you at newspaper after school today? I have a History test."

"I'll give you a hall pass," she replied sharply, not understanding that I really did not want to stay.

She pulled out a Post-it note from somewhere under her desk and a pencil from her hair, writing *Cassidy Fuller* underneath the words *hall pass 8:28* in bold capital letters. She signed it in a scribbly mess of lines that looked like a ball of yarn after it had been played with by a cat, so that the only letter that was legible was a big *M*.

She shifted her body forward, putting her maroon mug of steaming tea down on a pile of folders. I looked at the clock anxiously, but her lips curved, forming a small crooked smile, and her dark eyes seemed distant.

"Cassidy, I hope you know that you are an exceptional writer, and I have some exciting news for you."

"What?" I asked anxiously, as I leaned forward on my cushion, a little less worried about missing History. She always pauses like that for me to ask "What?" so she knows that I'm listening to her.

"Well"—she clasped her hands together in her lap—"there is a nationwide contest for little writers like you."

"Cool," I said, dropping my shoulders and doubting that I'd ever submit anything. Plus, I know that the high schoolers might look down on us, but I'm not exactly a *little* writer. Well, actually, I guess five foot three is pretty average for my age, but still. I usually don't like to share my writing with other people, and she had pretty much forced me to join the daily newspaper club. It wasn't bad, though. No one read it anyway, except when they were mentioned in it. Ms. Kahn was a little eccentric, but she was not strict or anything, so it was all right.

"I think you should give it a shot," she said, handing me a flyer crammed with words in a font so small that all the ink seemed to blend together.

"May the odds be evah in your fav-uh," she said in a bad attempt at a distorted British accent as she quoted the Hunger Games.

Chapter 4

"Oh, and there's a pretty substantial cash prize," said Ms. Kahn. That caught my attention. Elliott needed money for college, even though the scholarship money he could potentially earn would cover most of it. If I played my cards right, I could help him go to that music school he'd been telling me about.

Elliot would most likely be accepted to some of the best schools in the world. My parents wouldn't let him go unless he paid for it himself which they knew wasn't going to happen. They thought he was ruining his future. Plus, I know it was all partially because of Aunt Carol who *used to* sing every Wednesday at O'Reilly's, the Irish pub downtown. Even that wasn't a great gig though-not for a 50 year old still waiting for stardom.

Aunt Carol hadn't been all that steady financially lately, and I overheard my dad telling her to grow up and get a real job. He told her it was time to act like the older sibling for once and not to be so dependent on him. Until that night a few months ago when I heard them talking, I thought she was just staying in the guest room for a visit, but I guess I was wrong. Maybe she doesn't love us after all. Maybe she only sees us for the money she'll never earn on her own to help pay her bills and the home-cooked meals my mom leaves for her. But Elliott won't end up like that. I just know he won't.

He received a 2390 on his SAT and a 36 on the ACT, takes all honors and AP classes, and still has a 4.0 unweighted GPA. He set up a fundraiser to help the arts programs in a few of the poorer towns closer to Boston, has been on student council every year of high school, is editor of the school newspaper, won a state science fair last year and got to go to D.C. when he made it to national levels for a bridge-making engineering competition. And even though he says he's not much of a sports person, he used to run the two mile run in cross country in under ten minutes, winning almost every meet freshman year before he quit to make more time for orchestra practice. He could get into an Ivy League school if he wanted to, but he doesn't.

That's what my parents want—for him to go to Harvard for business and have a practical, office-working life like them. They say that all his hard work has been for nothing if he's just going to choose impractical majors, but they just don't understand. He doesn't do anything to get into what people consider a good college. He does these things for himself. Everyone acts like the college you go to determines your whole future. Not Elliott, though. He does things to build character, not to build a higher probability of getting into a good college so he can make a lot of money when he grows up, with a good job, and live a stable, intelligent "good life."

I think he would rather keep playing all of those instruments than be the richest person on earth. And that's exactly why I want to help him. He has passion, which is completely different from determination. Determination is trying and trying to reach a goal someone else sets, whether it be society or a specific person. Passion, on the other hand, comes from one's own heart. It's what people can't live without.

Too many people have determination without a passion.

Chapter 5

I told Ms. Kahn that I would be at newspaper club later that day and walked out the doorway with the pink Post-it note, starting to lose its stickyness, in one hand and the other arm carrying my books and binder with my notebook hidden between them. The hallways were almost as deserted and desolate as they were in August, when I had visited the soccer field next to the school with Summer.

Neither of us was very athletic, though, and we ended up just laughing and ranting about random stuff as we climbed under the shade of the sycamore tree until we could practically touch the scorching sun. I don't care if the topic is about the latest gossip, politics, or an argument about the best movie. At the moment, Summer says *The Sandlot*, but that's only because she is totally obsessed with the main character, Benny "the Jet" Rodriguez, and also because it's her dad's favorite movie. She is such a parrot sometimes. I personally like *The Dead Poets Society*, while Summer says it's weird to like something just because your teacher says it's good. It's kind of funny how one's perspective can differ so greatly regarding one place. On hot muggy August afternoons, the school is a place to hang out and sip fluorescent sour-green-apple Slurpees from the 7-Eleven down the street, but now, it's a building that tries to teach us as much curriculum as possible in ten months, with endless projects and tests. It reminds me of how I see Elliott as my best friend, but my parents see him as just some naïve kid missing his *Big Opportunity* at life.

It's weird to see this sentiment in print. I really don't think my parents are bad people or that they don't love us. I think they just show their love in an unnecessarily distorted way. They want the best for us, even if they don't know what that is. I can't exactly blame them when one thinks about the average starving artist. But my brother isn't average.

When I arrived at History class, I handed my hall pass to my teacher, muttering my apology quietly. I sat down in the back of the classroom sheepishly, hoping he wouldn't notice I had been late. Unfortunately, I came just in time for the start of the test, and my teacher threw the stapled pages onto my desk like a Frisbee, the papers fluttering like a white butterfly.

I had Science next. Elliott's pretty good at Chemistry and Physics, but I still don't understand them no matter how many times and ways he tries to explain it. And I'll definitely never remember the whole periodic table like he did by the time he was in sixth grade. I just don't understand how we're made up of so many cells and how those cells are just a compilation of atoms that have other parts made of quarks, and so on. Writing is so much easier. I do OK on the tests, though.

After Science, I had Spanish, which is really easy, even if I can't always remember which letters have accents. I think I like it because it's just a bunch of words. I think words are the most powerful thing in the world. They can be insulting and hurt someone, or they can melt away a person's self-consciousness with a compliment. Words share ideas and perspectives. They are used to make the biggest decisions of history, and they make people who they are.

Chapter 6

At lunch, I sat at a table for six with just Summer. We had been best friends since we were little. I can't even remember a time before I knew her. She's my next-door neighbor, but it feels like she's my sister even though we look nothing alike. Her parents never had another kid after her no matter how much they prayed for one. She has dark caramel-colored skin and curly black shoulder-length hair that outlines her round face. She was wearing a purple skirt with blue flowers on it with a lavender cable-knit sweater with frilly lace at the bottom.

The lunch lady stared at us in a mournful way, and I could tell she felt badly that we were the only people at a big table tucked away from the rest of the kids. I mean, I have friends, but I'm not as close with them as I am with Summer. They sit with us sometimes, but today, since a few classes are out on a field trip, it's just the two of us.

Usually, though, there's at least one other kid around. These are the kinds of people who only text me when they forget their homework. I can joke with them, but I don't make inside jokes with them. I haven't even been to any of their houses, except for Joe Nacka, who lives two doors down, and Lindsay, because we were partners for a book report once last year (even though she didn't even know *Call of the Wild* was about dogs, despite one appearing on the cover). These are people I've mostly known since I moved here, but they wouldn't know anything about my personal life if it weren't for this fact. Still, they're nice, and they keep me from being a complete loser who doesn't talk to anyone.

It's not always lonely to be alone, though. I added a quote to my journal that I carry around, even to lunch. "Quiet people have the loudest minds."—Stephen Hawking. Some people just don't understand that, though. We were filtered away from all the food fights and drama of immature middle schoolers trying to act older. From the outside looking in, where we sat, it was like watching a reality TV show. Summer gave me half a cookie, and we just sat without talking for a minute, watching some popular Queen Bee girls we could care less about, who were crying, their mascara smudging, while another one tried to comfort them. Apparently, Jack

Mendoza had just dumped Audrey Hanson, according to Eddie Oakley, who was at the next table over. He's best friends with Jack and was also unsuccessfully trying to get Audrey to calm down. You could see the guilt on his face for breaking up with her, no matter how bratty she could get. We continued our silence because I wasn't quite sure how to act, but I knew we would end up ranting about it after Summer gathered all the details, and she always did. I think it was supposed to be good news for us because it was so obvious Summer had a crush on Jack (mainly because of his resemblance in personality and looks to that guy from that Netflix show) and now he was available. It was like a scene from one of those classic chick-flick teenager movies that are always about some dork and the popular kids who bully her, and they are always shopping or causing drama. It's weird how I wanted to be able to say I didn't care about what was happening, but at the same time, for some reason I couldn't wait to see what they did next.

I sculpted a swan from the tin foil my peanut-butter sandwich was wrapped in, and zoned out for a moment. I examined the mural painted on the nearby brick wall, unblinking for a whole minute, and then returned back to my lost train of thought.

Though we do have both popular kids and nerds, and all of the people in between, our school is a lot different from the movies. We have many sub-cliques, none of which Summer and I are really a part of. For example, there aren't *just* popular kids. There are the girls on the best soccer team and the boys who wear jerseys to class on football game days. There are girls who are smart, pretty, and athletic, and the boys who are trying too hard to be the class clown. Then there are the nerds who aren't always smart. There are the kids who love Minecraft or Anime, and those who listen to bands no one's ever heard of. We don't identify with any of them, even the middle-of-the-pack kids who are a little of everything. We weren't quite at the bottom, but we certainly wouldn't be getting invited to any of Jack Mendoza and Eddie Oakley's "legendary" parties any time soon. Audrey Hanson probably didn't even know my name.

Chapter 7

While I was trying to map out of all the tables to sit at during lunch, Summer asked me if I wanted to walk to the quaint ice-cream shop near the school after the bell rang. We went there a lot, and every time I ordered a vanilla for me and a chocolate scoop in a waffle cone for Summer. I reminded Summer I had newspaper again that day, and I asked why she didn't join, though, I knew she didn't really like writing as much as I did. But she never tells me how much she loathes the essays we have to write in English class because she thinks she's going to hurt my feelings.

I pulled out the crumpled flyer from my sweatshirt pocket, kneading the creases on the lunch table as I started telling her about the contest. She asked me what I was going to write about. I told her I was still trying to think of something because it had to be perfect. The flyer said to write a short story, but that didn't help me at all. I needed a good idea, but instead I kept staring at the formatting guidelines. It didn't change the fact that I was stuck, but I continued to stare at the bullet points about the twelve-point Times New Roman font and double spacing like when I repeatedly opened the fridge, expecting a Thanksgiving feast to magically appear.

I pondered about it for the rest of the day, forcing ideas out of boring things. At newspaper, I told Ms. Kahn that I had decided to enter the contest. I gazed out the window, unable to concentrate, my mind overflowing with ideas. But I dismissed them all immediately. At first they seemed like they might actually work, but I realized that they were simply lifeless the second I clicked my mechanical pencil to write them down and my optimism escaped at the same rate as my eraser left new pink rubber shavings stuck in the groove at the top of my desk.

I watched the birds flying in a V-shape in the dull sky, filled with clouds like dark smoke billowing out of a factory. A few joggers passed by, and an elderly man, with wispy white hair and a face of deep lines from smiling as he read a book on the grass with a black lab next to him. Somehow, he reminded me of an apple core left out on the ground to rot. His face was wrinkled, but his clear eyes seemed to remember the days when he was young, when he knew each day could someday be a grand memory. I could think of the stories connected to all of those things, but they were not good enough.

I was supposed to be writing an article about the school musical, but it was impossible to concentrate. Ms. Kahn let us go ten minutes late because she forgot to check the clock as she reread the same book—again. She sure loves that book, for a title I had never even heard of, and I'm a fairly avid reader.

Chapter 8

I decided to take the shortcut home since I was running late. I usually chose the sidewalk, but it was starting to rain again a little bit—though really it was just orphans' tears, the light showers that fall even with the sun out as I waited for a rainbow to appear, my neck sore from looking up so much as I walked —so I trekked through a muddy path in the woods under the canopy of murky green leaves. I was the first to leave footprints, with the impression of my sneakers made into a labyrinth for ants. The path was covered in orange pine needles, cushioning every step, and populated by a huge boulder I used to stand on when I was little, like it was a prodigious mountain.

It was silent in the forest. There were no birds singing and no hikers. No one to help if I got lost or attacked by a swarm of bees or kidnapped by some axe murderer. It seemed to be a painting I had stepped foot in, and it was different from any other time I had been there when people were walking dogs and heading to their boats closer to the summer time. That's why it made an icy coldness crawl down my spine when I saw the smoke reaching for the sky, despite the rain, only a short distance from my house. I imagined the trail of ashes spread on my lawn like black snow. I imagined the tree house that I built with Summer, gone. I imagined the fields of wildflowers and blizzards of soft dandelion seeds in the meadows, gone. And then I imagined myself gone, swallowed by the orange flames licking my skin numb with no one to hear me. I imagined the feeling of fire wrapping around me, turning each thread of my clothes into singed ashes before reaching my skin, like the time I had burned my hand on the stovetop, but a million times worse.

Then I heard breathing, and it sliced through the silence like a knife. It wasn't just the wind like the monster sounds outside of my window when I was little. I stopped, frozen, and walked in a circle to find where the sound was coming from. I heard a sigh—a human sigh. I followed it and breathed in without exhaling for a little while, in shock. It was a girl. And she looked just as stunned as I. Neither one of us spoke, but the silence vanished anyway. My thoughts pounded as if they could break out of my skull. Her threadbare clothes were wet from the rain, and her hair, which was on the verge of forming dreadlocks, were soaked, looking a slightly darker shade of blond.

She wore a maroon Boston College shirt from the '85 Cotton Bowl, and the musty smell mixed with her odor of low tide and spoiled seafood. I remember Summer and Lindsay talking about how everyone had a different "house smell." Their conversations just tended to be weird like that. Once, Lindsay returned my jacket to me because it smelled like my usual distinct blend of Chinese takeout, ink from my pens, which always seemed to explode, and flowery perfume. Summer told me that the perfume smelled like a funeral home, which is strange because she was the one who bought it for me.

Scrapes could be seen from beneath the rips in her faded jeans. There was mud covering most of her sneakers too, so that the rest of her shoes blended in with the color of the black Adidas logo. We stared at each other for what felt like much longer than the reality of a few seconds. Among a million other thoughts, my mind raced back to my journal, and I thought of the word *opia*—the vulnerability of looking into someone's eyes. It was the best I could do to describe the scene. An intense feeling of shock lingered. I couldn't even feel my legs moving, but I knew what I was doing. I noticed that she had a pile of damp logs, with a backpack on the ground next to it, and pine needles and dandelion seeds drifting inside the open pouch.

The silence faded, but it didn't break. Sometimes people use the phrase "silence is broken," in books but the noises just become more noticeable or said aloud. For me, sometimes the noise seems even louder when there is no talking. That way my thoughts are louder, bolder, *mine*. I made a note to myself to add that to my notebook later—loud silence—

which would make for twenty oxymorons. The girl fidgeted a little, moving her feet frantically, shifting her weight from one leg to the other. We tried to break the eye contact, but failed. She looked so familiar, but I knew she didn't go to my school. My school was fairly small, and I lived in a small town in Cape Cod, Massachusetts, where I knew most of the people. After a while, I couldn't stand it. Her face was so familiar, but I didn't know how we could have even met.

Chapter 9

"Who are you?" I questioned bluntly, albeit in a soft voice, trying to mask my fear. Thinking back on that, it's kind of an awkward question to just ask a random stranger in the woods, but I needed to know if she was OK.

"What if you're some crazy murderer? I really don't think I should be talking to strangers," she said sarcastically, and I just rolled my eyes waiting for her response.

"Ruth Harrison. You?"

I thought of the name over and over in my mind, with a story on the tip of my tongue but not breaking free, like the stories I tried to conjure earlier while looking outside my window.

"Ruth Harrison?! You're alive."

"Yes, yes I am. And who are you, Little Red Riding Hood?" She was referring to my red hoodie and lunchbox.

I knew I'd heard that name before. Well, read actually. Ruth Harrison had been on the front page of my boring hometown newspaper, a publication I read even though there was almost never anything interesting in it, until Ruth Harrison's disappearance at least. From what I had read, she was an eighth-grade girl from Florida visiting her grandparents' house. Her family had been on a boat and had crashed into the rocks on a foggy, stormy night two weeks earlier. They never found any of them: the mom, the dad, the girl.

Until now. And "they" was suddenly me. Officials had found the boat, smashed in the front against a sharp rock that jutted out of the black ocean, which was like a dark sheet of glass, reflecting the dead trees' spindly arms and cheese moon. The story was even tracked on the TV news every morning for a while, but they gave up and their hope died. The police have too many cases like this, and it costs a lot to search. In fact, maybe their hope died a long time ago.

The saddest part is how the police forgot about the case, or at least the press did. But I never did. I have a good memory, and I can still remember the old-school photos of her on the news and in the paper, her pale freckled face hidden behind frizzy, blond hair, smiling ironically. I guess she still looked similar now but, at the same time, she looked like a completely different person. Her hair was no longer just frizzy, but messy, her complexion darker with new freckles lining her cheeks, and the smile and happiness in her blue eyes had faded.

"I figured you were dead," I said, not realizing the harshness of my question.

"So did I."

"What on earth is that supposed to mean?" I questioned, trying my best to keep my New Year's resolution, even at the easiest time to swear.

"I climbed into some stranger's yacht," she replied in a flat, bored tone, still not answering. "I've been sleeping there until yesterday when I ran out of food and jugs of water. It's not exactly a glamorous life."

"It's been, like, two weeks. And why didn't you just take a dinghy back to shore earlier or something?" I asked, while thinking of what it would be like to live on a yacht for almost two weeks. Even though I knew it was the Proctors' yacht (rich summer people who rarely visited in the winter because they were too busy at their ski house), I wondered what would have happened if they had found her.

She muttered "whatever" in a huff under her breath.

I didn't know what to do. She didn't seem like she wanted help, and I didn't want to help her, but at the same time I felt like I couldn't just leave her there.

"You want a bag of chips?" I pulled out my lunchbox, extending my arm to show her the snacks I didn't get to finish in school. Her eyes widened, but then she fidgeted with a necklace under her sweatshirt and said no.

"Aren't you hungry?" I stared at her fire, smothered by beads of rain, a tiny fish skewered on a stick over where the smoke once lifted. She said no again, but I could literally hear her stomach growling.

I quickly became tired of this and said, "Fine, but I have to turn you in anyways." In the five minutes that I'd actually known her in person, she finally showed some human emotion for the first time.

"No, please don't. I need to find my parents. When we crashed, they said they would just swim back to shore to get help for me. They told me to stay on one of the big boats in the moorings. They're coming back as soon as they find help," she responded, with panic rising up her throat. She turned around, pathetically trying to mend her fire.

"Wait. You need to come to my house. You can't live like this."

"Yes, I can, and I have." With this, I knew she was right, but I knew I couldn't live like that. I couldn't live knowing she was just wandering helplessly, like a goldfish trying to find the ocean from a glass bowl. She could survive, I was sure, but she couldn't live and do anything but the necessities. Plus, now she didn't even have an easy source of food and water, and there was no way for an eighth grader from Florida to make enough money even if she did find her way to the center of town.

Chapter 10

"I promise we'll find your parents. You can stay with me," I reassured her, even though I was pretty sure her parents had drowned already if it had taken them two weeks to swim the mile and a half to the beach in forty-degree water. We shook hands, and she followed me back home. I covered my head with my hands, but she just stared at the sky in a thoughtful way, letting the droplets shower her. Then she touched her silver locket again, actually smiling until I saw her, when she pretended nothing happened, turning her head the other direction.

When we got to my street, I could already tell from the top of the hill that my mom was home. I also knew that she wouldn't let Ruth stay. She was still clinging to the hope that Elliott would go to a "better" school than those music schools he'd been searching on his laptop, and Ivy Leagues are expensive—too expensive to account for another mouth to feed. I stopped walking, pausing, mid-stride, and saw my mom starting to pull out of the long driveway, carrying her big reusable grocery bag in the driver's seat.

Ruth asked, "What?" And when I mentioned how we couldn't let my mom see us or else she couldn't stay, she darted toward a few shrubs, hiding behind a full bush next to the cracked gray sidewalk without even saying a word. I followed her and, whispering, asked why she had run off without a plan. She told me that she was good at hiding and she'd done it so many times on the boat. When old men came in long trousers to go clamming, she would hide. And even in the day and a half she had been on land, she would hide from dog walkers and runners.

"Didn't you want to be found?" I questioned, confused.

She looked at the ground and plucked threads of green from the soil. "Well, I wanted to go home," she said, but with my family in my house, not a foster home. If they found me without parents, they'd write a few articles and throw me in a foster home. Both of my parents were only children, and all I had besides them was my grandmother. The whole reason we came to her house was to help clean out her stuff and spread her ashes since she had just died. That's why we were on her boat. We wanted to spread her ashes in the water, because she always talked about how she used to go to that specific spot by the lighthouse when my grandfather was still alive and they were young. She said the stars were brighter and more beautiful there, and you could see Martha's Vineyard behind the fog. She could go on for ages about it, and how the lights reminded her of *The Great Gatsby*, or how she once saw a huge sea turtle lost from its family. Mostly, we wanted her to be with my grandfather, and she had been the one who wanted him to have his ashes spread there."

I guess I understood, but it still seemed kind of weird. My mom passed by without even seeing us, and we started walking again. I pulled the key out of my jeans pocket and wiggled it, opening the door to a house of dark rooms, the lights turned off. The stairs creaked beneath our feet, mud trailing off her sneakers.

Elliott wasn't home yet; he was at the library tutoring some younger kids. As we passed his room, Ruth gasped at how heavily it was plastered in posters of bands and composers most people had never heard of, and I had never even heard of, until he played some of their music for me. When he grows up, he'll probably name his kids John and William, after John Williams, the guy who wrote the music for *Star Wars*, *ET the Extra-Terrestrial*, and *Jurassic Park*.

I opened the door to my room, and Ruth looked around at the desk: I had it covered in papers and a coffee mug of pens. She saw my twin bed with a quilt my grandmother made for me years ago, and my closet, filled with flannel shirts like the one I was wearing, and T-shirts with quotes on them or pictures of book covers. They limply slipped off the plastic hangers, so that my closet had a new "carpet" of colorful clothes.

Chapter 11

I told Ruth to sit down, motioning to the polka-dotted beanbag chair as I jumped onto my bed. I said that she could stay as long as my mom and dad didn't find out, since everything got them mad. She agreed with a silent nod of the head and, after trying to figure it out, we decided that we could set up somewhere for her to sleep in the drafty attic with insulation poking out of the walls like cotton candy. It wasn't perfect, but I guess it was better than a fancy-yacht-turned-cold-boat that smelled like fish.

I had her help me carry a sleeping bag, a pillow, and some of my clothes up the steep, creaky steps. There was an old couch up there too, but it was pretty disgusting, with stains and rips all over. I took off the cushions for a makeshift mattress. I laid the sleeping bag down like a picnic blanket and told her to go shower and put on the clothes I gave her while I started my homework downstairs.

I couldn't concentrate on History though. I was way too busy with the present (wow, that's cheesy). It was bizarre to consider that someday I would think back on this day and it would be history, and hardly the present. It would be separated from the rest of my boring days; maybe, in fact, this day would be the end of my boring days and change me forever.

In just one day, I had received an opportunity to help Elliott do what he actually wanted to do, found a girl in the woods, and had my life changed forever. I tried to copy notes for my project, but it seemed impossible to concentrate, and I started doodling instead. I made faint, quick lines to sketch Elliott's piano and Ruth's face, dotted in freckles and sporting an overconfident expression, and then I drew a pencil with my name, Cassidy Fuller, underneath it.

Ruth thundered downstairs in heavy footsteps, and I realized how much time had slipped away as she changed and showered. The dirt had vanished, revealing more freckles on her skin; her once frizzy, blond hair matted down into a sheet; heavy drops falling onto the oversized T-shirt and denim shorts. She had no shoes on her feet, callused, like her hands.

We sat down at the circular wooden kitchen table, and I laid out some stale crackers and lemonade, happy that my mom was finally going to the grocery store. I stared as Ruth gulped down lemonade full of stringy pulp and chomped a sleeve of crackers so old they crumbled on the ridged sides.

"Did you just steal that guy's old food when you were on the boat?" I asked, trying not to seem rude even though she was eating like a dog.

"I got by," she snapped. In the hour that I'd known Ruth Harrison, I had already learned a few things:

1. She did not feel the need for explanation.
2. She was independent.
3. She was a pig when it came to old Ritz Crackers.

I was genuinely interested in a response to my question, but I didn't even ask again, intimidated by her. At the same time, I felt I needed to help her every time she tried to be strong, and I thought her independence gave her enough strength to become vulnerable. I had so many questions, but I couldn't ask them when she looked down at me, even though she was only an inch or two taller than me.

Chapter 12

Recognizing the sound of his bad muffler and tires crunching the perfectly beachy sea shell driveway, I could tell Elliott was home. I didn't panic this time though, smiling inside while noticing Ruth's confidence replaced by a shot of fear in her blue eyes. It was the first time in fifteen minutes that she paused her feast. I stepped outside, feeling the rainfall on my back as the screen door shut behind me, waving to Elliott.

When we walked back inside, Ruth, hoping to become invisible, halted like the deer I often saw on my way to school early in the morning. Elliott waved to her casually, putting his backpack down to start on his homework in the living room. I was almost disappointed that I didn't get to use my cover-up story. Sometimes it scares me how good I am at lying, even if I view it as just writing without putting it on paper.

She exhaled out, able to breathe again, and we went outside to the music of rain in the gutters dancing on the thick lawn. A melody even more solemn plays in the backyard, where there is a shed full of intricate spider webs as an audience. The rusty lawn mower sat in the corner, remembering when it was bright red and put to use under sweat and sun during the summer. We crouched behind the shelter of two collapsible nylon chairs. I breathed heavily in the stuffy air, recollecting games of hide-and-go-seek at dusk.

"Why are we here?" Ruth asks.

"So we can talk about things," I answer, wondering why else we would hide in a shed in the pouring rain. "In private," I added.

"Yeah, whatever. You made it sound kinda urgent though. Plus, why can't we talk in another place?" she huffed.

I muttered "sorry" under my cold breath, wondering why she seemed so mad at me for no reason.

"What's your story?"

"I'm looking for my family, and it would save some time if you quit talking and helped me like you said you would," she answered. I couldn't tell if she was joking or not.

"I haven't done anything but help you!" I shouted louder than I ever had before, especially considering that I'm somewhat shy, even though I hate that word.

"What's with you?" I asked, not willing to lose my mind to the unexplainable aggravation that was filling my body. I breathed in and out, concentrating on the way my stomach filled with air and then released it. I tried to stay calm, but I felt like a raging ocean forced into a calm, dark blue sea without a ripple.

"What, are you, like, on your period or something?" she snarled.

"Are you? 'Cause you're sure acting like it!"

It was an ugly girl fight, and just thinking back on it makes the argument seem completely ridiculous. I mean, I fight with Summer all of the time, but in a best-friend sort of way, stealing her cookies at lunch after she trips me. And I fight with Elliott in the kind of normal sibling way, him telling me not to use sheet music as scrap paper blah blah bah and me playing pranks on him. But those end in laughter. They also end with the comfort of knowing it's all just a joke. This one didn't. It didn't leave me with that feeling either; it just left an ugly tension buzzing between us.

She looked disgustedly around the close walls of the shed and said, finally, "I thought I told you already. We were on my grandparents' boat so we could spread the ashes. We only had two lifejackets. But there were three of us. My dad gave one to me and one to my mom, even though we insisted for him to have it. After we crashed, they said to stay where I was. I perched on the big rock where we crashed, while they swam in to get help. I watched them, as they got farther away and disappeared from my vision, and the huge waves seemed to rise almost as high as the rock where I sat. I slept there with just the clothes on my back and a lifejacket, without dinner or breakfast the next morning, and with a dying thirst. So I went to the yacht, a diamond in the rough, and it became my new home. Sometimes I even called it Chappy, which was the name painted on the side of the boat. I was so bored I would talk to the boat and myself, because that was all I had."

By this time she looked startled, realizing how vulnerable she sounded.

"That's awful," I said without realizing she was probably trying to get me to feel sorry for her or else making stuff up. She shrugged her exhausted shoulders.

"So are you going to help me?"

"Yes." I didn't say *yeah* or *sure*, because I was serious. Her whole life's future had been dumped onto mine in a matter of minutes, almost like Elliott's, but on a larger scale. It was scary to know that, if I didn't help her, she could be miserable, an orphan, and alone.

"We'll start looking on Saturday."

She sighed but then agreed, and I could tell she may even have realized she'd been acting rude. It was Thursday now, which meant I had school the next day. It also meant that I had nothing to do with Ruth the next day. I couldn't just leave her home. I didn't even know if I could get her to stay that night. Telling my parents was not an option. She told me that if I told them, then she'd probably have to go to a foster home or something. I guess I only had one clear option.

Chapter 13

"You're coming to school tomorrow."

"What?"

"You're coming to school tomorrow. You can't just stay here," I repeated.

"I don't go to your school. I don't even live here," she reminded me.

"I'll just say you're my new next-door neighbor from…New York. Got it?" I slipped a Yankees T-shirt off a plastic hanger, and turned the logo toward her. It had been a gag gift for Elliott last year, a die-hard Red Sox fan.

She nodded, but it was not a strong nod. It was the kind of nod people do automatically when they want to create the impression that they're listening. Then I remembered Summer was my next-door neighbor. I would now have two next-door neighbors, but what would she think?

"Or you could be my cousin. I mean, we don't look all that different. You look more like me than my actual cousin, Erica."

Ruth opened the door to the shed, stepping onto the grass beaded in jewels of raindrops.

"Where are you going'?"

"Are we done." It was not a question, and I didn't respond. I just followed her back to my room. Elliott was too absorbed in studying to notice us as we trailed muddy footprints up the steep, creaky staircase to my room again. We had a lot of planning to do. I rolled my chair to my desk (where the chair is supposed to be tucked away) and opened the flap that hung over a rusty hinge that squeaked every time. I let my fingers linger midair, above my stash of notebooks, like I was Beethoven about to begin an interminable symphony, before selecting one. I plucked a sheet of paper out of one of the notebooks I didn't use as much, and the sheet tore off the binding with one quick rip. Ruth stared at my collection as I grabbed a pen to jot down "THE PLAN" at the top in sloppy, all-uppercase handwriting.

Not to brag, but I came up with a pretty good backstory. I added bullet points:

• Ruth is from Brooklyn, but her parents got divorced, so now she lives here in West Falmouth, MA

• Her mom works for an insurance company.

• Her dad is still in New York.

• She just moved here and is in all of my classes, so she's shadowing me for the first week.

I smiled at the bullet points, because I just created a whole life, and it seemed pretty believable.

I pulled out my wrinkled schedule, from the beginning of the school year, reaching the bottom of my backpack, shocked that anything could even survive that long in my black hole of a bag. She peered over my shoulder to look at it and told me she never took Spanish in her old school, like that's even a minor problem right now. I said just tell Señora Gonzalez that, and to keep calling it her "old school." So then, of course, I just had to make up some stories about her old school—like the time everyone in gym class refused to run laps and they all got detention; or the time she blew up the microwave in Home Economics class; or the one about the class clown, who pulled the best pranks on all the teachers. It made it sound more authentic.

I heard a rumble like thunder echoes through the air. It was my mom's minivan pulling into the garage. I told Ruth to go hide inside the attic where we had laid out her blankets, as I peered out the window and then ran down the stairs two at a time to help my mom bring the brown paper grocery bags into the kitchen from her trunk.

I snatched a bag out of her hands and one from the trunk and she took two more. I tried to take those too, but she wouldn't let me carry them all, not understanding that I was trying to slow her down. I stood in the doorway and asked how her day was, and whether she bought any of my favorite grape soda. I finally heard the heavy door to the attic slam shut, dropped the conversation, and started pulling boxes out of the bags to put in the refrigerator and cupboards.

After I brought in a few more bags, I mentioned I had a lot of homework to do, and I found the musty scent of the attic again.

Chapter 14

"My mom's home," I said. Ruth nodded.

"I can stay up here if you want. I told her I'm doing homework."

She replied, with "whatever" and a shrug of her shoulders. I took that as a *yes* and rummaged through cardboard boxes to find a board game or something. I blew the dust off some old photos and found onesies from when I was a baby. I stood, watching the small specks dance through the air against a golden beam of sunlight. Those beams shot through a window that looks like a porthole, illuminating the musty room. The heat was overwhelming, emanating from the pink, puffy insulation trying to escape the walls.

There was a picture of my whole family, sporting summer tans in Florida from a few years ago, and a few yearbooks and class pictures. There was one of my whole kindergarten class, and I became filled with an overwhelming nostalgia. Lost in memory, I noticed how all of the kids still had the same faces, but just smaller bodies back then.

Then I found a picture of Elliott when he was probably about my age, smiling as if he was about to laugh; smiling a real smile, as he sat at the bench of the keyboard he bought with his own money, cello propped against it. His face still looked the same, with dimples and brown hair gelled a little in the front. One piece always fell from his bangs onto his big glasses. I compared it to his other pictures and noticed he was not smiling in any of the other pictures—not truly smiling, at least. At a first, obvious glance, he was smiling, showing his teeth and his mouth curved upward, but his eyes were sad, the life faded.

Even though I saw the Scrabble board underneath a pile of books, I prepared a new idea instead.

"I need your help."

"I thought you were supposed to be the one giving help."

"This is what friends do. Friends help each other."

Ruth looked at me in the eyes for a few seconds and said, "Oh my God, sorry, but I'm not your friend. I barely know you. I just want to find my family."

The words hung in the air for me to comprehend, and it was loneliness, because loneliness is when you become comfortable with the routine of no one wanting to know who you are, your passions, your values, and what makes you unique. Today, I've learned yet another lesson. Rejection is worse than loneliness. It is failure.

Chapter 15

I scratched the part of my forehead right above my dark eyebrows, which don't match my hair, so that my hands covered my heavy, drooping eyes. My face flushed, slightly pink instead of my normal skin tone, and I breathed slowly, blinking consistently to hold back the flow of tears. I shut my eyes like I was trying to imagine a specific fact in the middle of a history test, and I tried to put on a brave face, but I couldn't. I cried. For the first time in what seemed like years, I cried. I had always expressed my writing by transferring thoughts and emotions into lines of ink in my notebooks. I did a good job too, never losing sleep over bad report cards or crying at funerals, dressing in black, where I could hide in the shadows, in the corner, as tissues were passed around. But I was crying in that moment, and it was all because of the words of some lost girl from the woods. I tried to say "forget it," my lip quivering, as I realized I hadn't even told her what I wanted help with. Nor could I even remember that I was just looking for some more story ideas, and I went to my room, leaving her to stare out the porthole window with a distant expression on her face.

I opened the wooden flap of my desk, revealing my abundance of various notebooks, and picked one, plucking a purple ballpoint pen from a mug. I opened the hardcover that was covered with quotes, but I didn't even read them. I usually think carefully about each one, but when they applied to my life, I didn't even give them a glance. I figured I could do this myself. I didn't need Ruth. She was the one who needed me. She just wouldn't admit it.

I wrote "My Entry for Martha" at the top, but it was a lie. I was not entering the contest for Martha, the quirky English teacher who gave me the flyer that was carefully folded up in the back pocket of my jeans. It was for Elliott. I had heard a lot of people say, "Write for no one but yourself," but I disagree. I don't agree at all. I wanted Elliott to live the life he wanted. I wanted him to live his life, and I wanted everyone to know what his life is, and who he is. My parents mean well, but they don't understand him, and I think that is the basis of every problem in history: misunderstanding. I didn't want to be the only one to know that I was a sister to a prodigy, a word which I don't use lightly.

He taught himself violin when he was only four. After seeing my aunt and the guy that used to have an empty case out on the corner of Maple and Main Street, he was determined to follow. And he did. He started subdividing rhythms before he could count to one hundred. He picked up piano a few months later, according to my dad's older sister, Carol. She's technically the only other person who knows these facts, but she lives in California now that she's taken some odd jobs-enough to move her out of our house at least. He used to watch her play when my family visited, when she used to live near us in Boston, in an apartment that was probably too small for her collection of instruments which was even bigger than Elliott's was. She told me he was better than her before he even started school. Now his room looks like the band room at school. I've lost count of how many instruments he plays by now, and I have a good memory. At least that's what everyone says. I think I just like to remember the small things, the tiny gears that make everything work and that's what helps me put together the big picture.

I stared at the lined pages, intimidated by the way they glared back at me. I was procrastinating with daydreams and checking my phone every other minute. I checked my e-mail and answered a few snapchats, but I was just stalling. I didn't know what to write. It was like I'd forgotten *how* to write. All I knew was that I really needed this.

It needed to be a fictional story, but there weren't many rules other than that it had to be at least a twenty pages. I couldn't concentrate at all, and I felt like a laptop with a million tabs open at once. I usually didn't have this much trouble writing. I usually didn't have those tears slowly drying on my cheeks or their salty taste lingering on my lips and leaving me feeling not just broken- but hollow, too.

Chapter 16

I decided to write in my diary. And by the way, this was not a place for me to scribble about how annoying popular girls were or how incredibly cute my crush was. My sight was blurry, my eyes wet; face red, swollen and snuffling. There was no other option. Most people talk to someone when they're sad. I write. It's a chance for me to speak without anyone judging the way I sound or calling me a whiny baby. I pulled out yet another journal, this one a black leather-bound book with a silky ribbon built in so I could find my place. With this one, it was much easier to write, and I didn't even care how sappy I sounded.

Dear Diary,

Today is March 12, and it has been a very eventful day. Mom and Dad were arguing with Elliott about college again (surprise, surprise). Then Ms. Kahn handed me this flyer with a really small font and made me late for class, and I really want to enter a story, but I don't have any ideas. Then, when I was walking home from school I found a girl, Ruth, who was on the news for a long time after her grandparents' boat crashed. She came home, hid from my family, ate my food, and made me cry.

—Cassidy Fuller

I felt different: not much better, but not worse. At least I felt clearer. I had it all written in front of me to assess. My eyes were dry, but my face was salty and stinging like when I go to the beach, which was only a bike's ride away from my house. I tried to forget, but I realized that wouldn't help if I was thinking about forgetting. I sat without moving for at least a minute, but my mind was still moving. (Sometimes I wish I could keep up with my head, but the thoughts come so fast that I can't focus on one subject at a time.) I was still thinking about how mean Ruth was after I let her come into my house. Didn't she understand that I didn't have to do this? And then something unexpected happened, even considering how hectic the day had already been.

The door to my bedroom sheepishly opened, as if it were pushed by a soft gust of wind. Ruth appeared from behind it, her straight yet frizzy, blond hair poking out before her face. Then she gained a little more confidence and walked up behind me. I tried to close my journal before she saw, but it was too late. This was worse than when my teachers snuck up behind me and caught me writing poems or observations about the world outside my window.

In school, I never hurt anyone. I think the teachers already knew I wasn't amused by their boring lectures. The lives around me were more interesting than long equations and historic events, which I'd given up on a long time ago. It fascinated me how everyone had their own stories, their own lives, their own worlds, just outside the window. Also, this happened to be one of the cool words I collected in one of my notebooks: *Sonder*—the realization that each random passerby has a life as vivid and intricate as your own. I just never expected Ruth to be one of those people.

She was the main character of her life's imaginary film, and I was the protagonist of my story too.

"I'm sorry," she said. She'd read what I'd written, and there was no way to fix it. Still, I tried to make it go away.

"What'd you say?"

"I said I'm sorry. I'm sorry I hurt you. I'm sorry you don't really want me here. And I'm sorry I'm a burden," she said, biting her lip with drooping eyes.

"You're not a burden," I said, trying my best to sound as sincere as I possibly could.

"Then why'd you write it in your frilly little diary?"

But it wasn't a question. Just then I realized something important. Words are powerful—I'd always known that, but I never thought there was another part to it. Words have the power to hurt people, and that's what I'd done. I didn't think Ruth would be hurt, but I was wrong. I was wrong about a lot of things.

"I'm sorry. I shouldn't have said that, but you really did hurt me. Why'd you say that?" I asked, even though I sounded like a lame kid from the health-class video about how to apologize properly.

"I think I just need to process things."

I nodded in agreement. It must have been weird to be living on a stranger's boat and on a random rock in the ocean independently, and then be forced to come back to some other stranger's house. I tried to change the subject after an awkward silence, one filled with loud doubts about whether this was even going to work.

"Want to go uptown?" I asked.

"Why?"

"Well." I stared at the baggy basketball shorts and oversized T-shirt reading Falmouth Road Race 2000 I had given her. Except that the race occurred before either of us were born. "I think we need to do some shopping. You know, clothes, extra food." She muttered "fine" under her breath and so, it was a plan.

Chapter 17

I grabbed the keys from the top of the dresser in Elliott's room, making a jingling sound as I rushed down the stairs. Ruth, confused, followed me. He was in the middle of doing homework, binders and papers spread out in front of him on the coffee table in the living room, the cool rocks I found from down the street securing the worksheets from the breeze rushing and rustling through the half-open window. He didn't even realize I was standing there until I tossed the keys at him, snapping him out of his trance. Then he just stared at me, waiting for an explanation, opening his eyes wider, and raising both eyebrows so his forehead wrinkled.

"I need you to drive us to the Dollar Tree."

"Wait a minute; I'm busy," he turned away. "Just let me finish this page."

I stood in the doorway with my arms folded in front of me for about five minutes. It was five minutes of silence. I was getting used to the bursts of silence and loudness, but at the same time, the silence spoke louder than when Elliott was practicing in his room, and the clear sound of a piano cut through the door and filled the house with its vibrations—or when Ruth snapped at me. The silence allowed me to think, and that was what I needed, as I climbed over the stair railing instead of taking the steps and impatiently waited for the garage door to open. I needed to do a lot of thinking. When he finished, I slammed the slightly rusted door of his gray car, rolling down the window of the passenger seat. I patted my jean pockets, making sure I still had the one hundred dollars I'd saved up as a collection from all my family for my birthday. That could buy me one hundred things at the Dollar Tree.

"You know, I'm not your personal chauffeur," Elliott said, sounding annoyed at first, but then breaking into a light laugh, eyes rolled and smile crooked.

"Sorry, but Ruth and I need poster board for our school project, and it's due tomorrow," I mumbled. It's scary how easily I can lie, but it's scarier that I can lie to my brother. "So it's like, really urgent," I added for emphasis. He said OK and that he'd be in the bookstore, which is part of the chain of shops that don't add up enough to really call a mall.

We opened the heavy glass doors, walking into the unorganized aisles of cheap Hawaiian leis, star spangled paper plates, and hair elastics. I pulled a small kelly-green spiral notebook out of my back pocket like a detective eager to take notes at the scene of a bloody crime. I flipped past the lined pages, so thin that I could practically see my fingers on the other side of the paper. I'd scribbled quotes that Elliott gets e-mailed to him from "quote a day", which was some website he subscribed to. He shows me, especially when it's one of my favorite authors or one of the scientists or musicians I've come to like because of him.

"So what should we get?" Ruth asked with a shrug of her shoulders.

"Well, what do you think you need?" She still seemed uninterested, and I started to list items, counting on my fingers.

"Food, clothes, shoes…" I made a bullet point in my list for each thing she didn't object to and grabbed a beige plastic shopping basket, scanning the aisles before deciding what to add. She followed behind me. I held up a pair of white sandals with a lot of straps crisscrossing plastic rhinestones. She shook her head no. Holding up a pair of violet flip-flops she shrugged, "These are OK." I added them to our basket, content that they only cost a dollar. I figured that her sneakers were practically falling apart, the rubbery soles splitting from the rest of the shoes caked in dried-up mud.

Then we found a green-and-white-striped cotton beach cover-up that was passable enough for a dress. There weren't really any pants available, so we picked out another cover-up-style dress, almost exactly the same as the last one, except it was completely green. Anything was better than the baggy, navy blue basketball shorts and dated T-shirt she had on now.

Then again, I didn't exactly know anything about fashion. I wore jeans or leggings and oversized T-shirts and my favorite blue sweatshirt or green military jacket every day, the sleeves threadbare from me leaning on them all the time, especially when writing, like at lunch when Summer wasn't at school. There were thumbholes in all of my sweaters from balling up my fists when I was feeling particularly shy. And I always wore my Converse high-tops, which were white when I bought them but became an unidentifiable hue somewhere in between white, brown, and gray, with my weird socks underneath hidden by my jeans.

I sighed and decided we had to move on to food, which was like trying to find a decent meal at a gas station on a road trip. Except it went on for what seemed like days. There was a value pack of Kellogg's cereal and some stale-looking granola bars, which ended up being the most nutritious things we found. It's not like we were looking to be health freaks anyway as we strolled through the aisle of theater style candy boxes and the freezer full of Choco-Tacos near he cash register. We added a few Hershey's bars, Ritz Crackers and lemonade in the kind of juice pouches that have holes to put the yellow straw through. Still, I looked for some decent food and knocked over the trail mix, revealing some sweatshirts and T-shirts that said "Cape Cod, Massachusetts" in puffy, white letters, as if any tourist would shop for souvenirs at a Dollar Tree store. (Plus, they weren't even a dollar. Five bucks was still cheap, but I think it's false advertising.) Ruth tugged a few off their plastic hangers and threw them into the basket without even folding them.

I watched the way Ruth's sneakers printed muddy stains on the store's square pieces of orange carpeting, and we started to unpile our things onto the conveyor belt. I looked up to see the old lady with a perm of hair the color of a dull pencil lead staring at us. In her defense, it looked like we were moving into the store with all the stuff we had.

Right as she stuffed everything into beige plastic bags, I saw Elliott cupping his hands around his dark eyes against the glass windows. I noticed that all the other stores were closed, and the intense, glaring lights overhead made the place seem like a mirage in the desert. The parking lot was almost empty, and the streets were eerily desolate. I shooed him away, with my fingers in a quick flutter, as he held up his watch with his free hand, a Barnes & Noble bag in the other.

"Thank you."

"What?" I said, turning my head to Ruth.

"Thank you," she repeated. "Thank you for buying this stuff. Thank you for letting me stay with you. Thank you for being my friend."

I had been surprised a lot that day, and that was one of the biggest moments of all, but it was interrupted. I didn't even get to thank her or tell her that she was my friend, too (which still seemed weird given I'd known her for only a few hours, but she felt so familiar). I just let the words hang in the air like they did two hours earlier when she wouldn't accept my friendship. Words always hang in the air like that when something is powerful. They slice through wind and ring like clear bells in a Christmas carol.

Chapter 18

Elliott walked through the doorway, saying, "You were supposed to meet me in the bookstore ten minutes ago."

I didn't remember this at all.

"Sorry," I mumbled, even though I was not sorry. I was not sorry I made him wait "ten whole minutes." I was sorry that Ruth tried to be nice to me, to be my friend, and I rejected her.

"Whatever," he said, dismissing it in a short huff. "So did you guys get everything ok?" he asked, pulling open the car door.

"Yeah," I lied.

"Why'd you get so many bags? I thought you only needed poster board."

"Well, we got some candy," which wasn't completely a lie.

"Don't tell Mom." Then I remembered he probably wouldn't talk to her anyway.

"Is she still yelling at you about school or whatever?" I asked my brother, putting my sneakers on the dashboard, my jeans drooping behind my ankles so my socks with the giraffes would appear. I accidentally knocked over his Yoda bobble head and ignored it as it fell on its side. He looked at me like it's a stupid question—which it is. Sometimes you have to ask the boring, obvious questions to get the interesting answers. That's another thing Elliott taught me. I'm too blunt, which I still don't think is a bad thing. Instead of asking, "Why are you crying? Did you fail the test or something?" I should ask, "Hey, what's up? How was your day?" I still think that's pretty pointless.

"Dad, too," he added. "They say they want the best for me, but they don't know what that is. They don't even know me. They said I have to grow up, I'm such a bright kid, but I'm not acting like it. They think I'm stupid; my dream is stupid and that I won't earn a decent living."

"Smells like *teen angst!*" I yelled in a low voice like a television announcer. That's our inside joke for when Elliott gets moody and deep.

"Oh shut up, Cass." He rolled his eyes, but I knew he didn't actually hate that joke that much because he used it on me all the time despite it being out of my time.

"Oh," I said, like when I'm on the phone with someone and don't want to keep talking so I don't bother to ask any questions. I don't even care that it doesn't make sense in the context. It's not that I'm uninterested, but Ruth looked uncomfortable. I would be too, but he didn't know what she had been through.

"They don't understand though. I don't care about the money. I've worked too hard to give up; to give my passion up to be normal. Why should we revolve around money like planets around the sun instead of our dreams? Dreams are clouds. They can rain at any moment, with the power to be a thunderstorm or a puffy cumulus nimbus."

I cut him off because I was listening, even if he sounded like some freak who's trying too hard to sound deep (which he does a lot). I held off on my teen angst joke for once, even if the timing is perfect.

"But it's always sunny without clouds."

"Who says sun is good?"

He took a hand off the wheel to make hand gestures. But they're not just hand gestures. I recognize these movements. He was conducting to the classical music station he sometimes forced me to listen to. Right now, it's this piece he says is really hard, but he wants to get it down before the high school band goes to some festival in New Orleans during April vacation. It really is pretty. A whole symphony coming together in one united voice like a human organ, with the sweet melodic whistle of the flutes and increasing tempo kept by percussion. If he doesn't become a musician, I bet he'll be a conductor.

"Dance in the rain. Make a splash," I turn away from Ruth and look at him, laughing. I don't really know where he gets these things. I can tell he's coming down from having his head too far in the clouds. He always does eventually. There is a long pause, and that's when I am sure he is conducting. His right hand slices through the air with a precise rhythm. His hazel eyes become distant behind his big glasses, but he is focused. When he is finished, he finally says, "Sorry, I don't think I've introduced myself. I'm Elliott, Cassidy's brother. Who are you?"

"My name is Ruth, if that's what you mean."

He says, "I did not ask your name. I asked who you are," but not in a rude way; rather with his easy awkwardness and random pauses.

I wrinkle my forehead and furrow my eyebrows, squinting as I hold her gaze before she turns away. It is a silent pact. We promised each other not to reveal who she really is.

"It's kind of hard to explain," she starts, but she doesn't look me in the eye. "Cassidy and I never were, um, like, working on, uh, this project thing." She starts uneasy at first, the words stuck. "I don't even go to her school. I haven't been to school in over two weeks. I lost my family after my grandparents' boat crashed, and Cassidy found me on her way home from school. She said I could stay. For a little bit, at least."

Chapter 19

Elliott turned around, his eyes widening as he realized she was the girl he saw on the news. She was in the paper, and her picture was posted on the wall of the supermarket for her fifteen minutes of fame in our sleepy New England town.

It all happened in less than a minute of a moment. Moments are not measured in time, and I had a feeling this was going to be a very long moment. It was a moment that started with an end, like many beginnings do.

He jerked on the brake, and I plunged backward in my seat. But there was no red light casting a ruby shadow. A second later, I was stricken by the impact of a huge airbag. It shot at us like a soccer ball hurtling at a hundred miles per hour before I could even comprehend that they had deployed. The echo of our screams droned out the sound of cars beeping, as I coughed up the powder that helped aid the airbags and burst out with them. We'd swerved into a metal guardrail, and the driver's side window shattered in a million pieces like glistening snow. Seconds later, the airbags had deflated again, leaving burns on our chests and shoulders.

It was all a blur immediately, even though it had just happened. I'm trying now to forget, but it's not working well enough. My mind was racing and blank at the same time.

"All right?" I yelled.

"I think so," Ruth said, glancing at the cuts dripping with blood on her legs and arms. I said "good" even though it wasn't good. It wasn't good at all. I was still coughing in between words while inspecting the red blotches on my skin.

"You?" she asked.

"Yeah, I'm fine," I said, trying to catch my breath. I had slammed into the side door. It was a numb pain, and I could already picture the bruise forming all over my shoulder. Elliott stared at his hand with a loss of breath. The tiny pieces of glass were punctured all the way up his arm, and his hand looked even worse. He squeezed his eyelids in pain as he tried to make a fist, but he couldn't.

"Holy shit! Are you OK?" I said in shock. I felt like the words didn't belong to me —that they shouldn't have belonged to me. But they did. The whole scene felt like a nightmare come to life.

"We should probably get out," Ruth said after what felt like a while, but in reality, was probably just a few seconds.

The sirens of an ambulance shrieked, rushing toward us. It took Elliott away, and I pleaded that we were fine. Messing with us would only take time away from him being treated.

That was when I called my dad. He left the house as soon as I told him where we were and what had happened, but I left out the part about Ruth and how it was partially her fault and also partially Elliott's fault. I knew that I was the one to blame though. I was the one who brought Ruth home and forced Elliott to drive us to the store.

My dad didn't care about that though. He just wanted us to be all right, and he rushed us to the hospital, the trees on the side of the road flashing by in a blur. At least we were lucky that he was working from home that day.

I don't remember much else, even though everything seemed so vivid at the time. So clear, and so confusing. It was like time had stopped and then started again in full speed to make up for the lost time.

I tried to keep hope, to keep my head held high, but it felt nearly impossible. We read a poem by Emily Dickinson in English with Ms. Kahn, a.k.a. Martha, but I couldn't hear it, no matter how many times I repeated it in my head. It became a variation of words when I needed it most.

> *Hope is the thing with feathers-*
> *That perches in the soul-*
> *And sings the tune without the*
> *words-*
> *And never stops-at all-*
>
> *And sweetest-in the Gale-Is heard-*
> *And sore must be the storm-*
> *That could abash the little Bird*

That kept so many warm-

I've heard it in the chillest land-
And on the strangest Sea-
Yet, never, in Extremity,
it asked a crumb-of Me.

I tried to listen, but I was interrupted. It was a pounding in the back of my head, ready to break through my skull. But I wasn't ready for it to be more than a thought, to be a reality. *To be my life.* Even the sirens ahead of us couldn't drone out my thoughts.

I sat in silence, but it was louder than real silence. My mind was wilder than any conversation ever could be. I tried to tell myself everything was going to be all right, but I knew the truth and no amount of repetition could wash that away. The truth is always there. Sometimes it's just more buried than others.

I knew I should have felt lucky we'd all survived. And lucky that we didn't hit another car. And lucky that my dad picked us up. And lucky that someone had called an ambulance. But I felt anything but lucky.

Chapter 20

"I'm sorry," said Ruth.

"It's OK," I said, even though it wasn't. Nothing was OK, but what was I supposed to say?

"No, really," she said, cutting through my train of thought. I looked up, but avoided eye contact, my lip quivering, and my hands shaking uncontrollably.

"It sucks. Just when you think you know your life; you know yourself—it's all ripped to pieces. You think they'll be there forever. They'll be there for you, but then it's impossible for you to even be there for them."

I didn't say anything. I didn't know what to say. She didn't exactly do me a favor, so I guess "thanks" wouldn't work. It didn't even hurt when she told me the thing I had tried so hard to hide from myself. So I just kind of nodded timidly. That was the last thing she said before the beginning of the end.

My dad didn't hear. He was listening to me explain what had happened, and he had a lot of questions. He wasn't mad, but he seemed concerned.

When we got to the hospital, Ruth and I sat in the waiting room, pretending to flip through glossy-paged gossip magazines, even though we weren't exactly reading the exaggerated headlines in bold white font. I bounced up and down against the wooden armrests of the blue-cushioned chairs. Families held hands with a firm grip, strong as their love despite tears escaping their tightly shut eyelids. In a way, I wanted to be one of them, to be a part of something, but then I remembered. I remembered what they were held together by: the glue that stuck the pieces of their dying hearts into one.

I never thought that Ruth would be the one to start the puzzle of dying hearts, but she didn't need a family with her to be human. Staying quiet never meant you were strong; it was expressing yourself.

Her tears were like a thunderstorm. They started with only a drop, but then grew into puddles.

"It's all my fault. I bet you wish you never met me," she said, trying to stop her voice from wavering. And that was when the mist became a hurricane. I could feel my face getting hotter, my cheeks turning pink like a sunburn, and my nose getting runny. It wasn't until I started to cry that I realized I was sad.

The shock lifted like fog and with it the confusion. I had never cried. Not when my arm broke in third grade or when I got an F on an essay in English the previous year, the one thing I didn't suck at. I think I was saving the tears for the waterfall of now.

"It's not your fault," I muttered after a long pause.

"Yes, yes, it is. You know he stopped like that because of me. It was just shock."

I couldn't argue with her, because I knew she was right. Even if I told her how the rain was heavy, and that the car was too old, she wouldn't have cared.

"It's OK. It's not your fault. He hasn't even had his license for a year yet," I said with drooping eyes.

"But what if he's not OK?" she answered, looking at her muddy sneakers. I didn't have anything to say.

I looked at the families around us, trying to solve the puzzles of their shattered hearts. And then I stopped watching. I stopped watching and became one of them, and I gave Ruth a hug, patting her on her wet back below her rain-soaked hair, which was starting to frizz like wispy cotton candy after a hot shower. At that moment, it didn't matter if we were in the midst of a tragedy, because I had help. I never noticed how lonely I was until I had more true friends who understood me. More than just Summer, Elliott, and Ms. Khan (and Summer was the only one I could really call a friend and still seem normal).

Then a nurse flashed an artificially white smile and told us we could go into Elliott's room, so we followed her. It smelled like shoe cleaner, the pungent aroma penetrating my nose in hallways filled with old people hooked up to oxygen tanks and sick children visited by clowns carrying poodle balloons. They weren't the kind of people I ever thought Elliott would be associated with. They'd been forgotten as people until they were just patients, surrounded by masses of "get well" cards from strangers. But they had stories too. I wondered if any of them were prodigies like Elliott or writers like me.

Chapter 21

Ruth and I walked into his room quietly, the nurse behind us.

"I'll leave you alone," she said, and left without another word.

He was asleep. I wondered how he could look so peaceful. I glanced at the clock in disbelief. It was already seven o'clock. I figured he had taken some medicine or something that made him tired.

After I sat down, his eyes slowly fluttered open.

"You OK?" I asked impatiently as soon as he woke.

He looked at his cleaned scars, saying, "I might not be able to play again."

"What do you mean?"

"I have something called boxer's fracture in my hand. Plus, I can't even bend my elbow. The left one. It might be paralyzed if the glass cut down to my nerves. Dad already signed the waivers, and mom's talking to the nurse or something. She was just here a minute ago."

"But what about your music and all?" I asked.

He looked down at his hospital bed and gown and replied, "Gone. It's all gone."

And then Ruth cut in. "No. I've never heard you play or anything, but a little birdy told me you're some kind of musical prodigy," she said, smiling at me.

"We can fix this."

After a while of watching the news on the tiny TV, high on the wall, the nurse came back.

We weren't allowed to join him for the operation because Ruth wasn't part of the family. I wouldn't be able to hold his hand for the last time. No guitar for him to strum sadly. No piano for him to play, the clear sound ringing softly and loudly at once. He couldn't play any instrument now, and that was what he did best. He was good at a lot of stuff, but talent is different from passion.

I tapped my hand against my thigh, making the beads of my bracelet jingle up and down, and Ruth flipped through the channels. After some searching, she landed on *Judge Judy*, but I couldn't watch.

The room was almost too clean. It had a window, and you could see the roof where sparrows flocked to. Mostly, I remember that there was a lot of space, yet nowhere to feel comfortable. They had given him a nice room, and I figured that was a bad sign.

My mind was always full of stories that never had clear-cut chapters. They usually merged one into the next, like watercolors on a wet piece of paper, the paints expanding until they faded into one another. I've heard people refer to events as the beginnings of chapters in their lives: graduations, weddings, anything really. But it's not like that. Life is just a progression from each moment made of tiny moments. Now it seemed like I was trying to read five novels at once.

I sat in silence. And I found out that is one of my very few talents (the others include: writing, my impeccable sense of fashion for socks, dislocating my toes on command, lying in emergencies, and bending paper clips into every letter of the alphabet). Some people go insane if they don't have anything to do or anyone to talk to. I am not one of those people, nor one of any "people." My thoughts offered the discussion of millions, and I had a lot to think about and more that I hadn't even started to think about yet. What would happen with the insurance? Did we even have insurance? Would we have to pay for destroying the guardrail? Did my mom know about Ruth yet? Would Elliott get a prosthetic arm? I would've sat there for hours if I hadn't been interrupted.

I heard a short ring from Elliott's phone, which rested on the table next to his bed and was covered in pamphlets about what to do if someone has a heart attack or a stroke, and a menu for bland hospital food that arrived on blue plastic trays like in the school cafeteria, and consisted mostly of rice, green beans, and red Jell-O for dessert.

Ruth turned toward me, glancing away from *Judge Judy* for the first time in a while, as I opened his e-mail. A *number one* stood above the envelope icon in front of his screensaver, an image of the two of us with Aunt Carol, when she took us to see the Boston Pops on the Fourth of July. That was two years ago, when Elliott had a real smile.

Chapter 22

I scrolled down the list of e-mails growing impatient at the sight of the loading sign. There was another e-mail—a very important one. Actually, they were both very important. It just depended on who you were.

I guess my eyes must have widened like a deer in headlights because Ruth decreased the volume on the tiny TV, massaged her neck, and asked "What?"

"Elliott got two e-mails."

"So?" she said.

"I don't think I should open them."

"Whatever. They're probably just spam anyway. Just open them, what does he care?"

"They're not just typical ads. They're important."

I could tell she became more interested, as she turned off the TV completely. "Where are they from?" she asked, leaning slightly forward from her chair on the other side of the hospital room.

"Carnegie Hall and Harvard."

She didn't say anything. And she didn't need to. I knew that those two e-mails had a lot more to do with his fate than one would think.

"Open them!" she said with shaking urgency.

"Are you sure? What if they're private?"

"Open them," she repeated, walking over to my chair next to Elliott's hospital bed, my thumb hovering on the sticky home screen on his phone, still unsure if I should just exit

Gmail. She leaned over my shoulder as I pressed on the one from Carnegie Hall with a shaking hand. My eyes scanned every word as fast as possible.

Dear Mr. Elliott Fuller,

I am writing to inform you that you are cordially invited to play at Carnegie Hall. We were very impressed by your application video, and would like you to come play on April 15. I will send you a letter in the mail with more information. In the meantime, keep practicing piano and have a song prepared.

Sincerely,

Elena Bloom

"That's so cool! I wish I was good at something," Ruth said, smiling. But when she saw my expression, her smile faded to match mine.

"Oh, yeah" she said, remembering the obvious.

"Can he play with just one hand?" she asked, clinging onto a thread of hope I'd become blind to.

"Nope. At least not well."

I could tell she was still scheming, but I moved on to the next e-mail.

I searched for the few words in the long letter from Harvard that mattered. The pretentious and verbose lines blurred together until one thing was clear. The one thing that was important; to everyone but Elliott. I wondered if he would even care that he was accepted.

Chapter 23

I slumped in my chair because I understood the undeniable truth.

"You know, he's not going to be able to go to Carnegie Hall, and my parents are going to force him to go to Harvard. As if they hadn't been trying to make him go there the whole time."

"Stop being so negative. Have you heard me complain once because I fricking lived on a boat by myself and got in a car crash just for you to end up whining to me," she screamed, fighting herself not to raise her voice even higher.

"Sorry…" I murmured in a whisper.

"No you're not. You haven't asked me once about myself." She didn't say anything after that.

I had never even noticed Elliott had a roommate until a boy about his age, but much taller and scrawny with shaggy spikes of red hair, pulled back the curtain dividing the room in half. They looked similar somehow though. Sure, Elliott was five feet ten with neat brown hair, but maybe it was that distant look in their hazel eyes. I also didn't see, until he pulled back the curtain, his wheelchair, covered in bumper stickers for the British TV show, *Doctor Who*. And then I glimpsed at his missing right leg. I tried not to stare, but I could tell he noticed, as he gave me a sad smile, and then he looked down at where his leg once was and at the stump that replaced it. "You're Ruth Harrison," he said to no one and everyone.

"And…?" she answered, completely unaware of how often her picture was shown on the news and the search parties that looked for her.

"You were on the news a lot," he said, unphased by her bluntness, which I was just starting to understand.

"I guess they found you then, huh?" Some of my neighbors and I went to look for you guys. I live right next to the trail."

Ruth looked at me, searching my eyes for what to say. When I didn't answer, she responded, "Umm, yeah."

"I'm Wilson," he said, wheeling his chair closer, stretching out a thin, pale arm before staring at our cut arms and shaking hands with us awkwardly.

"This is Cassidy," she said, gesturing toward me.

"Well, nice to meet you, Cassidy," he smiled. "What are you guys in here for?" he asked genuinely.

"Well, we were in a car crash," said Ruth.

I added, "Yeah, but we just got a few scratches," because Wilson probably thought that's nothing compared to missing half of his leg.

"My brother injured his arm. He should be back soon though. The nurse told us probably a few hours. All the tests and x-rays are taking a while too."

"Sorry to hear that. That must've been pretty scary. How old is he? Was he driving?"

"He's almost eighteen, and yeah. How'd you lose your leg?"

Ruth elbowed me in the gut, harder than she intended to, and I mouthed, "Sorry."

"Bone disease. I didn't lose my whole leg though. Just part of it."

"Sorry about that," said Ruth.

"Really, don't be. I mean I get this snazzy chair, a bed with a remote, and some gift-shop chocolates. It's all good." He forced a smile, and then turned to the window overlooking the ocean far away, behind the wall of white pines and cottages. He didn't avert his eyes from the wall until Elliott came in, with my mom and dad behind him.

Chapter 24

My mom kept scratching her arm, and my dad played with his ring so that his small tan line showed. They never said that they were scared or nervous, but I knew they were. I also knew the only reason they didn't say anything about it was because they didn't want me to be more scared. They thought that was their job as parents—to be brave.

Ruth walked behind me as I fell into my brother's warm hug with only one arm lifted.

My parents didn't even notice that I was with her.

"You're OK," he whispered serendipitously and gratefully. I nodded in unison with Ruth.

"You're not OK, though," I said, staring at where the splint was, his whole arm wrapped like a mummy in gauze. "It was my fault anyway." Ruth didn't even argue.

Wilson shouted, "Hey, Elliott. I'm Wilson."

"Hey."

I explained to him that Wilson was his roommate, and that I told him all about Elliott. Wilson rolled his chair next to Elliott's bed. Elliott lied down, declaring that he was tired but that he could still talk a little. He told Wilson it had been a long day. I don't think that even comes close to surmising the day's scenes, which played in my mind like a movie theater filled with a million films.

I decided to leave them alone, remembering the way Elliott would sometimes get embarrassed by me when I was around his friends, but wouldn't tell me. I told them we were going to the cafeteria, but Elliott just nodded without saying anything. My dad went to talk to the nurse, because he's the kind of person who doesn't see anything wrong with bombarding busy people with a million questions. And my mom just sat, alternating between tapping her feet and tightening her ponytail of short graying hair.

When we got to the cafeteria, I realized, as I reached into the pockets of my jeans, that I didn't have any money. I pulled out my phone and, when I pressed the home button, it showed I had a missed call from Summer, my next-door neighbor and best friend. I told Ruth we needed to go outside so I could take a call, and she replied by saying the food didn't look great anyway. It's really not much better than the food at school.

Chapter 25

I sat on the marble steps outside of the lobby with the friendly lady at the desk. They reminded me of the cold walls of a mausoleum, and I drifted off, staring at the parking lot, wondering how many people died every day in the hospital. I don't think I would want to be a doctor.

I dialed Summer's number quickly while pulling my knees to my chest. It rang for a while before she picked up the phone.

"Hey, got your message," I said.

"Oh, yeah. Your mom told me to call you. She asked if my mom could pick you up, because she's busy somewhere, and she won't be home for a while. Then she just hung up because she had to go sign a waiver or something."

"Yeah, the hospital," I respond.

"Oh my God! What happened?"

"Oh, it's kind of a long story," I laughed.

"Are you guys OK?" she asked.

"Not exactly…" I answered. I could imagine her pacing and finished my sentence. "I'm OK, but Elliott's hand might be paralyzed. We were in a car crash."

I tried to sound calm, but even the voice inside my head was shaking.

"How'd it happen?"

My mind was flooded by a blurry scene of the moment, trying to fast-forward, but always getting stuck on the worst parts like a scratched DVD. I could see the blood rushing out of my arms, and then that seeming like nothing when realizing how bloody Elliott's arm was. I had never seen that much blood in my life.

"Hello?" said Summer. I realized, snapping out of my trancelike state, that I was still on the phone. I blinked my eyes for the first time in what was probably half a minute.

"Oh, yeah. Elliott was driving, and then he swerved onto the side of the road. He just slammed on the brakes for no reason."

I left out the part that he only stopped because he was in such shock from discovering the person riding with us was Ruth, who'd been all over the news. I felt bad, remembering our pact never to keep any secrets from each other. But it wouldn't hurt her to not know, right?

"I'll leave in like ten minutes. My mom just has to finish cooking dinner, so she can turn the stove off. Are you OK with macaroni?"

"Oh, yeah. Thanks," I said, realizing how hungry I was.

It was already pretty late, and I knew Elliott had to stay for a while. I might have asked for the doctor's opinion on the cuts on my arms and legs as well as Ruth's. They were painful and bloody, but not as painful as watching my brother's life unravel in front of him.

A few minutes later, growing impatient with waiting, I texted Summer. I began strolling through the bright, sterilized hospital halls with hand-sanitizer dispensers around every corner to go say good-bye to my family.

I got into the silver elevator, which showed me from every angle within its smooth reflective surface. Ruth stood in the corner with her back to me. She gazed at her reflection, fascinated by the girl she hadn't seen in over two weeks. We didn't have enough time for her to change, so she still had on the baggy gym shorts and T-shirt I'd given her.

"Summer said she'll pick me up in a few minutes," I announced from the doorway.

"OK. I have to stay here a few nights. Bye," said Elliott, waving.

"Bye." I gave all three of them a hug, and then returned to Ruth, standing idle in the hallway.

Ruth and I walked out to the stone steps once again and waited there in the dark. There were puddles on the parking lot pavement, but it was not raining anymore. We sat down and waited for Summer to come, but it felt like ages. I laid down on my back, not caring that it was moistening my shirt, wet from the raindrops resting on the stone steps. I stared at the stars and wondered how people can possibly see constellations in the white specks, peeking out of the black abyss, like a flashlight shining behind a black blanket with a bunch of tiny holes in it.

Chapter 26

Suddenly, I remembered something very important. What do I do about Ruth? I asked myself. I hit my forehead with the palm of my hand, wondering how I could be such an idiot.

"My friend's mom is coming to pick us up," I said.

"Oh, OK," said Ruth. She probably already overheard me saying it anyway.

"But she doesn't know about you," I answered.

"Oh…" she said, realizing.

"What should we do?" I asked.

"We could just say I'm your friend from school, like with Elliott," she tried.

"But, why would you be at the hospital with me?"

"Oh, yeah…"

"Do you want some money for a cab?" I asked. I fished in my pockets, finding the cash that was missing when we were at the cafeteria. There were these white taxis for tourists around here with pictures of cartoon seagulls. They seemed out of place though.

"Thanks," she said, taking the bill I gave her. I didn't actually know how much a taxi cost, but I thought a twenty should be more than enough.

I looked up Falmouth Taxi and called the number, letting her talk. I told her to wait for me at home, and that my mom said there would be pasta on the stovetop. Ruth told me the taxi would be there soon, and gave me back my phone right in time, as Summer and her mom pulled up.

I got into the green minivan, but it was not until we were well onto the main road that I told them the whole story.

"I think Elliott's arm is paralyzed."

The words hung in the metallic-smelling air, distinctive of the way it feels after the rain falls. I still couldn't believe it, but she didn't seem to care.

"I thought he was just in a splint. Oh, God. I hope he's OK."

When they dropped me off I went straight to my room, slamming the door behind me. I flopped face down onto my bed, trying to sort out my jumble of emotions. I didn't even know what I was feeling anymore.

I lay thinking until Summer texted me.

"R U there?"

"Yeah," I answered.

"Want me 2 come over?" she asked. I thought in my head how badly I wished she could, but instead I said no.

I was taken aback as she texted, "Why not? You can't possibly be busy already. You just got home."

"It's nothing," I answered, but that was too much of a lie and more defiant than I really was. I knew that it was Ruth, but Summer couldn't know. We made a pact.

"I guess with Elliott and all…"

I thought that was good enough but then she wrote, "No, it's been the past few days."

"I dunno. I've been babysitting almost every day this week, and I had to catch up on homework since I was sick last week."

I lied again. I didn't know why she was getting so uptight in the first place.

And then I wrote.

"Why don't you just come over."

"K."

I felt relieved for a little bit, but then I realized I was going to have a lot of explaining to do. I also realized that Ruth would be very angry.

And then Ruth stepped through the window like they do in the movies, after climbing up the makeshift tree house we made in between the two houses. Except she's a lot less like a ninja.

I told her that I was going to tell Summer everything.

"What?" Ruth cried.

"It's going to be OK."

"No. No, it's not. You said no one would find out!"

"Well, it's been a while, OK. Didn't you think someone would find out at some point? What does it matter if I tell Summer?"

"But you promised."

"It's for the best," I said.

"I have to go."

She stared at me with a face of disgust and murderous eyes like the hollow ones of a shark. With her arms folded, she spun dramatically on her heel and faced the window where she had climbed through in the first place. Then she climbed out.

I saw her dart through the grass back to the woods. But I wasn't even shocked. I thought about her all the time, but there was nothing I could do. I thought about looking for her, but I knew, even if I found her, she wouldn't want to come back with me anyway.

Chapter 27

Two minutes later, Summer climbed through the same window. She had a backpack on her back and a sleeping bag. She was already wearing her pajamas. Shadows crawled over the dark complexion of her face, with a halo of brown curls hugging her cheeks.

"So what've you been doing that's kept you oh-so-busy?" she questioned. I could tell she had started to cool off. And then I lied.

"Well, you know how I was going to enter that story contest?" I said. She nodded, and I kept going.

"Well, I really want to win, but now Elliott's lost his arm anyway. Well, I mean, he didn't completely lose it, but…" I trailed off. "Plus, I was having a hard time working on it," I added.

"I'll help you," she said.

I said, "Sure," opening my desk, the hinges creaking as I pulled out a blank notebook from my collection.

"So I was thinking it could be about a girl who crashed on a boat during a hurricane and lost her parents, but then she went to go live with another girl who finds her on her way home from school," I explained. "I don't quite know how it will end, but it will come to me someday."

She was enthusiastic about the idea, and so was I. I finally had an idea. Ms. Kahn always said to write truthfully and to write what you know. In the story, I changed my name to Carla, anyway. We stayed up all night, the glow of the computer screen chasing away the darkness until the sun came up. I looped through my playlist a few times. My favorite songs felt better and more personal as they replayed for the third time. I submitted the story by e-mailing it to the address on my information sheet with a tired hand, and spotted Summer asleep on the couch next to me. It was at that moment of dawn that I felt loneliness the strongest out of my mix of emotions.

In the morning, after breakfast, Summer asked me if I wanted to go to the rope swing. My mom let me miss school since I had been up so late the night before, and she knew that I was really concerned about Elliott. Plus, I still had minor burns and bruises as an excuse. I assumed Summer was just skipping. I reluctantly said yes, even though it was next to a pond in the woods—the same woods where Ruth was.

We strolled through the woods, bedded with fallen orange pine needles. Summer had a soft smile on her face that managed to make her huge brown eyes look squinty, but my hand shook as I tapped my thigh.

We got to the rope swing and swung on it a few times, the wind ripping through my bushy brown hair, which I hadn't even run a comb through in two days. We took turns flying over the pond near the cranberry bog and then back to the dirt ground again, staining our bare feet as we skidded back. It must be like that all the time for the two white swans who sat in the still water. After a while, we went home, having still not found Ruth.

Chapter 28

A few weeks later, it was time for Elliott to perform at Carnegie Hall. I had e-mailed them that he wouldn't be able to play, but they never responded. So with Wilson's car (Wilson had a prosthetic now, so he could drive, sort of) and a backpack full of sheet music and peanut-butter-and-honey sandwiches for the long drive, Elliott, Wilson, and I left just like that, without a word to anyone else.

Loud Silence

I guess Wilson and Elliott had become pretty good friends during their stay at the hospital. Elliott told me that they talked a lot because the only people around, outside of my parents and me, were his best friend Blake, his girlfriend Alessia, Aunt Carol, and Ms. Kahn. Apparently, Martha found out why I was out when my mom called the school. She dropped off some candy for both of us and a note for me about my piece, which she had read in one day.

When we arrived, lights shone on the stage, creating beads of sweat on the other performers. The whole entire place was overwhelmingly hot. The seats were packed, audience members busy scanning the playbill. I went backstage with Elliott, but Wilson couldn't make it because it would be too hard for him to climb the stairs.

We looked all around for the lady from the e-mail. When we found her, she turned around, whipping her bob of blond hair.

166

"Yes?"

"Hi." Elliott shook her hand. "I'm Elliott. I was in this car crash, you see. My arm can't really move, and it might be paralyzed. We'll see—I mean, I have to go back next week for more x-rays."

"I see," she said with a stern face. She shook her head. "I just don't know what to do. You were supposed to perform ten minutes from now."

"OK," said Elliott.

"OK, what?"

And then he walked off. We found a ramp to bring Wilson backstage. Then my phone beeped once again.

"Was that yours?" Elliott felt his pockets.

I proceeded to read it. But it seemed so surreal, like time had stopped.

"I won," I said to Elliott in an emotionless tone. It only made me think of how bored Ruth sounded when I first saw her. "I won the contest," I repeated.

He beamed, and I wondered how he could be so positive.

"That's awesome!" He didn't ask what the prize was, but I told him anyway.

"But you can't go to your music school now," I said, not realizing how insensitive that was until the words fell out of my mouth. "And—" I said, as I continued to scroll, "I have been disqualified."

I could feel the sense of defeat in my own voice, but inside I knew I should've read the fine print. According to the rules, writers were prohibited from writing about a true story, as the contest was for a short-fiction book.

He frowned for the quickest moment, and then he smiled again somehow.

"I got accepted to Harvard."

"But you're not going, right?"

"I think I've had a change of heart."

"What? I thought you weren't even going to apply."

"Science and Creative Writing double major. Oh, maybe I could write for a Science Magazine or something. I'll figure it out as I go. I'm learning from the best." He winked with a corny expression. And at that moment, I knew he was not talking about Harvard. He was talking about me.

He walked onto the stage confidently. He waved with his right hand, but he didn't sit at the piano like he was supposed to.

"Hi, I'm Elliott Fuller. I know I'm probably going to get into some trouble for this, but I promise I will not be wasting your time." He cleared his throat, unaware of the blond lady glaring at him. He seemed so insignificant, standing there on the monumental stage under the high ceilings. "My good friend Wilson helped me write this speech, and I've learned a lot from my little sister, Cassidy. So here it goes, I guess."

The audience members exchanged confused looks as he began.

"I've spent a lot of time helplessly trying to find a good metaphor for music. I've found that throughout my years of practicing music, these metaphors have constantly changed. The one thing that has stayed consistent was that music is extremely important to me. I thought it was like a journal, and I could uncover things about myself as I worked on it. I thought it was water, and I needed it to survive, and it was a versatile ocean. But what I learned when I wasn't able to play anymore is that it is a metaphor for life—in a sense. It crescendos through emotions with unexpected staccato outbursts that you wouldn't suspect. Losing the use of my arm was like that for me, but I gained a lot from it. I also learned that music doesn't have to come from a sheet of paper filled with a neat staff and notes placed on the lines. I am still making music because I am still living. More staccato bursts like this will come my way. They could be good. Or they could be bad. I have to wait and see. So, to conclude, I want each one of you to remember to keep composing your masterpiece. Keep living, and if you succeed with this, your notes will ring true in your legacy decades from now, even if they are only the favorite melody of one person."

He walked off the stage as the stern blond lady glared at him again. I gave him a hug and whispered that his speech was beautiful and that I could see him as a writer. And then I let go.

"Ruth's very angry, you know."

"What? Why?" he asked.

I blurted it out all at once. "She's in a foster home now until they find her new adoptive parents, and it's all my fault. The people from the writing contest found out about her because I didn't change the names. She just called me today."

"She's in a better home now," he reassured me.

"No, no, she's not. I just wish she'd never left."

"Maybe she'll get adopted."

"Her parents are dead. She knows it too. She didn't want to admit it, but I heard her talking to the sky," I announced. I'll never see her again. I'll never be able to apologize for the contest and beg her to forgive me.

We got in the car and just changed the subject. I almost forgot about it, until I got the millionth e-mail of that month. It was from Summer. "Hey, can you help me set up? The foster kid's coming today. My parents have been waiting for someone forever, and there's finally someone. Plus, she's a girl our age."

"Sure. When?"

She responded in a moment, typing. "Whenever you can. She's coming next week."

"Yeah, OK. I'll meet you later."

Then she added, "My mom said we should be extra nice to her. Both of her parents just died a few weeks ago."

It was the perfect cheesy coincidence. I imagined a light bulb flashing above my head as I pondered a world with Summer *and* Ruth, living together peacefully. I thought of the Thanksgivings together, which had always been a tradition between our two families. I could imagine lunch less lonely and life happier in general.

Of course, I didn't even know if it would be Ruth. The odds were against it. But even the slightest chance of it made me hopeful and excited, the kind of experience to look back upon with rose-colored lenses. All of a sudden, the girl who had made me cry was promoted to my mental best-friends list. She was not my best friend like Summer, and she never would be, but she was one more person who made my days more entertaining and worthwhile.

I guessed this would be the next chapter in my life, even though I didn't love that phrase. It was an ending and a beginning all on its own, and I hoped it would be just like the chapter I just had. With all the ups and downs, summed together, this past one was good. I could feel the next one would be great. But chapters are not measured by the personal gain of the characters, but rather the plot, so I guess I would have to wait and see.

I smiled to myself, still lost in a thoughtful, loud silence as Wilson pulled into our gravel driveway. Summer and her parents were carrying a mattress into their house, with boxes and bags filling the trunk of their car. The windows were open, and I imagined the office where we used to have our cardboard-clubhouse building transformed into a bedroom. I could see its walls plastered in posters of bands and a desk full of homework pages fluttering in the wind.

"Bye, Wilson."

"Good job today, Elliott. You sure are one brave little soldier."

"See ya."

We just laughed with big goofy grins on our faces, waving good-bye to him as he honked the horn a gazillion times for no reason.

I smiled because I was a musician, and I knew this was just an accented outburst in my personal masterpiece. It was short, and it would pass, but it changed the whole piece. It might not be a perfect life, but it was a perfect song.

Acknowledgments

This book would not have been possible without the help and the support of my family, friends, and teachers.

Thanks to my parents, John and Monica Christo, who were the first to read my story and have always supported me. Thank you to my sister, Gabriela Christo, who helped me remember my target audience and encouraged me throughout this journey.

Thanks to my amazing English teachers throughout the years who've inspired me to love reading and writing and encouraged me to do more outside of the classroom: Ms. Hurley, Mr. Gavaghan, Mr. Gagne, Mrs. Sieber, and Mrs. Garcia.

A special thanks to my Third Grade teacher, Mrs. Interrante, who first introduced me to my favorite thing in the world, writing.

Many thanks to my Fifth Grade teacher, Mrs. Cowell who provided support and encouragement at an early age with special activities like The Poetry Cafe and reading books that made me want to touch someone with my writing the way those books inspired me.

Also, thank you to the Medfield Public School System, which has helped me stay curious, appreciate education, and enjoy school.

Thanks to Mrs. Erin Moran McCormick, who taught me all about publishing and inspired me with her own book, "Year of Action".

Thank you to Ted Murphy who made writing fun at the Just Write It Camp located in Falmouth, MA. The people there made a seemingly solitary and quiet hobby even more enjoyable.

Thanks to all my friends for supporting me, with the simplest words of congratulations, or even better, genuine excitement, sure to brighten my day.

Thanks to Lisa McDonald for helping me get out of my comfort zone and take pictures for the back cover of this book with ease and pleasure.

Also, thanks to CreateSpace. This wouldn't have been possible without you or any of the others listed above.

About the Author

Carina Marie Christo currently lives in Medfield, Massachusetts. She is fourteen years old, though she first started working on *Loud Silence* when she was thirteen. She likes to play field hockey, hang out with her friends, and write, of course! Follow her on Instagram and Twitter @carina_christo to see more of her writing journey and check out her website www.cmchristo.weebly.com or you can also email her at christocarina@gmail.com for comments or questions.

39397429R00103

Made in the USA
Middletown, DE
13 January 2017